This book belongs to

To Edward and Poppy
S. N.

For my wife Heidi –
your love and cuddles keep me strong
D. H.

First published in Great Britain in 2005 by Gullane Children's Books
This paperback edition published 2006 by

Gullane Children's Books

185 Fleet Street. London EC4A 2HS
www.gullanebooks.com

3   5   7   9   10   8   6   4   2

Text © Sarah Nash 2005
Illustrations © Daniel Howarth 2005

The right of Sarah Nash and Daniel Howarth to be identified as the author and illustrator of
this work has been asserted by them in accordance with the Copyright, Designs and Patents Act, 1988.

A CIP record for this title is available from the British Library.

ISBN: 978-1-86233-609-4

Printed and bound in China

The Cuddliest Cuddle in the World

Sarah Nash • Daniel Howarth

GULLANE
CHILDREN'S BOOKS

Mummy's gone hunting. Leopard is
left at home. Leopard is feeling lonely.
He misses Mummy and he
misses Mummy's cuddles.

"What's up, Spottychops?" says Bear.
"No Mummy," whispers Leopard sadly.
"How about a hug to cheer you up?" suggests Bear.

"AAAA … OUUCHHH … GET off," chokes Leopard.
"Your … hugs are muuchhh too tight!"

"Sssshall I give you a ssssqueeze?" hisses Python.

"Stop it..." giggles Leopard. "Your cuddles are far too tickly."

"Climb up here for a snuggle,"
calls Monkey.
"Help . . . let me goooo . . ."
screams Leopard. "Your cuddles
are much too whooshy!"

"Sha … ha … ha … ll I give you a
cu … hu … huddle?" chuckles Hyena.

"Yeuch!" splutters Leopard.
"Your cuddles are too licky."

"I will embrace you . . ."
smiles Crocodile.
"Ouch . . ." yelps Leopard.
"Your cuddles are
so snappy."

"Can I give you a huglet?" whispers Spider.
"Oh no . . ." smiles Leopard.
"Your cuddles are way too small."

"Oh dear," sighs Leopard, "I do miss Mummy."

"Listen up, Leopard,"
cries everyone,
"Mummy's back."

"Hello, little Leopard," says Mummy,
"did you miss me?"
"Mmmmm... and your cuddles..."
sighs Leopard.

"You give the cuddliest cuddles
in the world!"

Other Daniel Howarth books for you to enjoy...

I Love You Always and Forever
written by Jonathan Emmett

Longtail is faster and clever than Littletail. But that won't be forever, says Longtail. Then he tells her one thing *will* stay the same, *always and forever*...

•

For Everyone to Share
written by Gillian Lobel

Little Mouse has never been out of his nest before and he is thrilled by the sights and sounds outside. But what is this amazing place – and who is it for?

•

Santa's Little Helper
written by Angela McAllister

Rufus is playing hide-and-seek, and a big brown sack seems the perfect place to hide – until he finds himself flying through the air in Santa's sleigh!